Dear Violetta,

happy dreaming!
Love, Molly xx

MOLLY ARBUTHNOTT

ILLUSTRATED BY AGNES TREHERNE

OSCAR THE FERRY CAT

FIRST EDITION
- 2017 -

Edit & layout Shaun Russell

Published by
Jelly Bean Books
Mackintosh House
136 Newport Road, Cardiff, CF24 1DJ
www.candyjarbooks.co.uk

Printed and bound in the UK by
4edge, 22 Eldon Way, Hockley, Essex, SS5 4AD

Oscar was a Siamese cat.
He led the life of any ordinary cat.
He ate, he slept, and he sometimes caught a mouse.
But one day his ordinary life would change forever.

It was holiday time.
Nearly everyone loves holidays.
Everyone apart from Oscar.
He hated them.

Being in a hot car for hours was not fun. So, he ran up to the attic and hid. Soon, though, he felt two hands around his tummy, lifting him into a basket and out into the car.

The journey was very long, but suddenly the car stopped. Oscar spied an open window. He pushed open his basket door, crept over a suitcase or two and hopped out.

Freedom!

But where am I? Oscar thought.
He looked around and could see lots of ropes.
He listened and could hear waves splashing and seagulls calling.
"I must be on a ferry," he said.

The world outside was rather big and
scary, but Oscar could smell a mouse.
He ran under cars, around wheels and over ropes.
Where was this mouse and where was his car?

Oscar was lost and, with a roar,
the cars started moving.
The wheels were very big and
Oscar was very small.
“I want to go home,” he cried,
as he drifted off to sleep.

In his dream he was tapping a door.

Tap … tap … tap.

He woke up but the tapping didn't stop. There, right in front of him, was a seagull with a huge crab in her mouth.

The seagull hadn't noticed Oscar and was startled when he moved his paw.

So startled that her mouth flew open and out fell the crab.
"It's gone," she said. "Just my luck, I was looking forward to that."
"Sorry," Oscar said, feeling slightly guilty.
"Don't worry. It happens all the time. My name is Sammy the seagull. Who are you?"
"I'm Oscar the cat."
"Why do you look so sad?"
"I don't fit in here and I want to go home."

“Come and be a ferry bird with me? We’ll have lots of fun,”
Sammy suggested. “Hop onto my back and I will show you.”

Oscar crawled onto the back of the seagull.
He clung on tightly with both his paws, and up they went.
“Look how beautiful it is,” Sammy squawked.“Can you see the
cormorants diving for fish and the dolphins jumping?”
Oscar didn’t reply. His paws were getting wet and he felt quite sick.

"Where to now?" Sammy asked excitedly.
"That's very kind of you but I am not a ferry bird.
I am a cat and I want to go home," Oscar replied.
"Suit yourself." Sammy cried as she flew off.
Oscar curled up into a ball and cried himself to sleep.

He was woken by a snuffling sound. "Hello," a voice said.
"I'm Robert the rat. Who are you?"
"I'm Oscar the cat," Oscar replied.
"Why do you look so sad?" Robert asked.
"I don't fit in here and I want to go home," Oscar explained.
"Come and be a ferry rat with me. We'll have lots of fun," Robert suggested.
"Follow me and I will show you."

Robert led Oscar over lots of green, smelly, barnacled ropes and through holes towards the kitchen. “Look at these delicious scraps,” Robert said as he hopped into the rubbish bin. “Would you like to join me?”

"No, thank you. I only eat mice really," Oscar replied.
"Suit yourself," said Robert as he plunged back into the bin.
Oscar was alone again. "I'm not a ferry bird. I'm not a ferry rat.
I am a cat and I want to go home," he whispered.

But before he had time to think a
large black boot knocked him over.
"MEOW!" he exclaimed.
"Sorry, I didn't see you there. I'm
Charlie the chef. Who are you?
"I'm Oscar the cat," Oscar replied.
"Why are you so sad?" Charlie asked.
"I don't fit in here and I want to
go home," Oscar replied.

"Come and be a ferry chef
with me. We'll have lots of fun.
Follow me and I will show you."
Oscar followed him into the kitchen
and watched as Charlie started
cutting some vegetables.

"Would you like to try?" he asked,
passing Oscar a knife. But poor
Oscar nearly chopped his paw off.
"I think I should go," Oscar said.
"Suit yourself," said Charlie.
"Your tail is in my salad,
so please could you move?"

Oscar slipped out of the door. "I'm not a ferry chef. I'm not a ferry rat.
I'm not a ferry bird. I am a cat and I want to go home," Oscar said
as he curled up into a tight ball and went to sleep.

He was woken by a loud horn booming. *What is that?* he thought and went off to investigate. A man dressed in a white uniform was standing behind a wheel and blasting a horn. “Excuse me,” said Oscar, not forgetting his manners. “Please could you stop that noise? It is giving me a headache.”

"Oh, hello, who are you?" Colin
the ferry captain asked.
"I'm Oscar the cat," Oscar replied.
"Why do you look so sad?" Colin asked.
"I don't fit in here and I want to go home,"
Oscar said.

"Come and be a ferry captain
with me. We'll have lots of fun,"
Colin said. "Follow me and
I will show you.
This button lets other boats
know that we are here. It makes a
loud noise in the fog so the
boats don't run into us. Would
you like to try?"

Oscar reached over with his paw but the button
was too small and no sound came out.
"How about steering instead," Colin suggested.

Oscar tried his best but couldn't get a good grip on the wheel, and the ferry started going around in circles. "Maybe I should take over again," Colin said. "I will never fit in here," Oscar replied. "I'm not a ferry captain. I'm not a ferry chef. I'm not a ferry rat. I'm not a ferry bird. I am a cat and I want to go home," Oscar said, looking quite sad. Colin scratched his head. "OK, there is someone I would like you to meet. I'm sure they'll be able to help. Follow me."

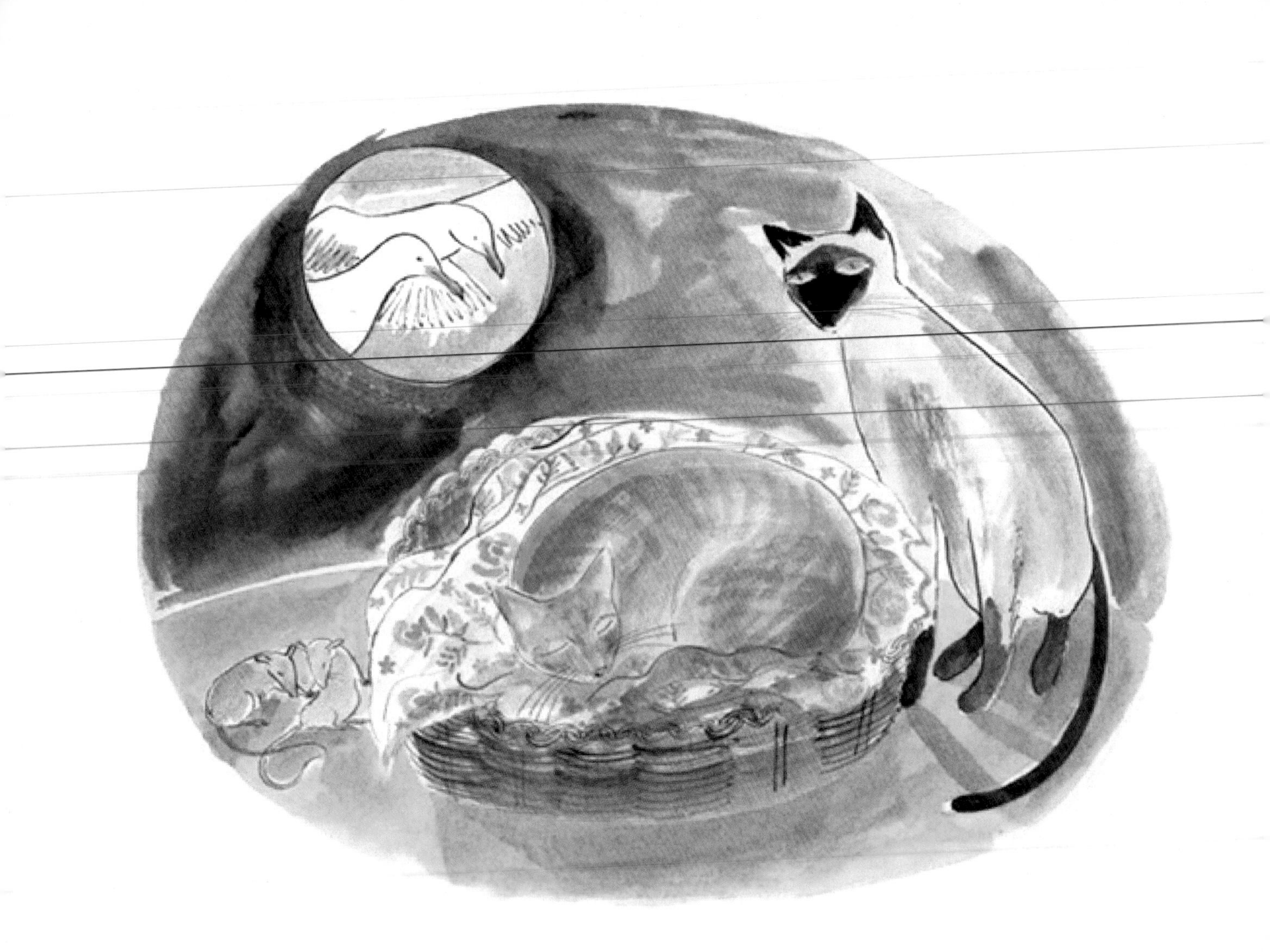

Oscar followed Colin down some steps towards a little door.
"Go through there," Colin told him, "and see what you see…"
Oscar slowly crept through. Sleeping in a flowery basket
was the most beautiful cat he had ever seen.

The cat opened one eye and said, “Is someone there?”
“Yes,” stammered Oscar.
“I’m Mercy. Who are you?” she asked. “I am Oscar and I am a long way from home.”

"Don't run away," Mercy said. "Come and be a ferry cat with me. We'll have lots of fun! Follow me and I will show you." Oscar thought for a while and then said, "OK!"

" I can't wait to share and enjoy Oscar the Ferry Cat *with my four-year-old great granddaughter and very much hope that we shall be treated to more of his adventures in a second book."*

Mary Sheepshanks, author

"I love the illustrations and the conversations with various new friends."

Rosamunde Pilcher

"A beautiful story with exquisite illustrations."

Abi Elphinstone, children's author